j

Pullman, Philip, 1946-

Spring-Heeled Jack
c1989.

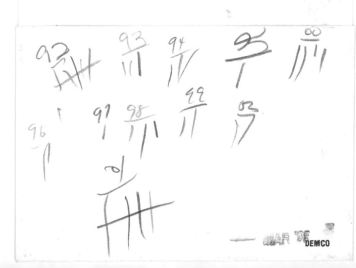

Spring-Heeled Jack

BY PHILIP PULLMAN
illustrated by David Mostyn

Alfred A. Knopf　New York

Library of Congress Cataloging-in-Publication Data
Pullman, Philip, 1946–
Spring-Heeled Jack / by Philip Pullman. p. cm.
Summary: Three children make their escape from a London orphanage
and after a series of misadventures are reunited with their father
through the efforts of the legendary Spring-Heeled Jack.
ISBN 0-679-81057-9 (pbk.). — ISBN 0-679-91057-3 (lib. bdg.)
[1. Orphans—Fiction. 2. Adventure and adventurers—Fiction.
3. London (England)—Fiction.] I. Title.
PZ7.P968Sp 1991 Fic—dc20 90-5151 CIP AC

THE LEGEND OF SPRING-HEELED JACK

In Victorian times, before Super-man and Batman had been heard of, there was another hero who used to go around rescuing people and catching criminals.

This was Spring-Heeled Jack.

No one knew what his real name was; all they knew was that he was dressed like the devil, that he could leap over houses with the help of springs in the heels of his boots, and that any evildoer who came up against him met a very unpleasant end.

Naturally, a character as mysteri-ous as Spring-Heeled Jack had a lot of stories told about him. And when people heard that Spring-Heeled Jack had been seen, they stayed in-doors and didn't look out of their windows. Because he *might* have been a man, and he might not. And some of his deeds were a little too devilish for comfort . . .

For Tom

CHAPTER ONE

"It was a dark and stormy night . . ."
Alexandre Dumas, *The Three Musketeers*

It was a dark and stormy night. In the city of London the wind was tossing the boats on the river and driving the rain down every alley, up every flight of steps, and in through every broken window.

No one was out if they had any excuse to stay in. No one respectable, that is. Only alley cats and criminals had any business in the streets that night, and even they took cover when they could.

High up on the third floor of the Alderman Cawn-Plaster Memorial Orphanage, though, something was stirring.

5

Rose, Lily, and little Ned had been in the Alderman Cawn-Plaster Memorial Orphanage for eighteen months, ever since their father's ship had sunk in the Indian Ocean. He'd gone to seek his fortune in the gold fields of Australia, and he'd never been heard from since. Their mother had died soon afterward, and the children had been taken into the Alderman Cawn-Plaster Memorial Orphanage, where the porridge was as thin as the blankets, and as cold as the smiles on the guardians' faces. No wonder they wanted to run away.

The only thing they had to remind them of their mother was a gold locket on a chain. Rose had it still, in spite of the rules of the orphanage, which said that children should give up any jewelry they had to the guardians.

But they'd had enough.

Spangle was quite happy to go with them. There wasn't much love where she came from, and the children had some to spare.

They huddled themselves up against the rain and the wind, and hurried off through the dark streets toward the Docks. At least, they thought they were going toward the Docks, but the streets were so dark, and the night was so foggy, that very soon they hadn't the faintest idea where they were.

They settled down in the doorway. What a place to sleep! Fog Row was the dirtiest, dankest, miserablest spot in the whole of the East End—and only a spit and a stride from a certain bunch of garbage cans.

And so they settled down to sleep.

The trouble with that particular bunch of garbage cans was this:

This was Mack the Knife, the most evil villain in London, and the garbage can concealed the way in to his secret hideout. There'd never been a more evil man than Mack the Knife. Cats fled, rats fled, policemen fled, murderers fled when Mack arrived. He was the King of Crime.

Oh, the folly of youth, thought Mack the Knife, climbing out from behind the garbage cans. How innocent they are! How simple! How lucky I am!

And he bent down low, trying to spot a gleam of gold in the shadows.

All of a sudden Spangle pricked up her ears and smelled him.

"You thief! You villain!" yelled little Ned. "That lock-et's going to pay for our escape to America!"

"No, it ain't," said Mack the Knife. "It's going to pay for a meat pie and a bottle of brandy. Now hand it over."

"Never!" cried Ned.

And he and Spangle threw themselves at Mack the Knife, punching and kicking and snarling and biting and spitting, and it did them no good at all.

But with Rose to one side and Lily to the other, and not knowing which of them had the locket, Mack the Knife was foxed. If he went after Lily and Rose had it, he'd get nothing; but if Lily had it and he went after Rose, he'd still get nothing.

On the other hand, he had Ned already.

They just didn't know what to do.

"Don't give it to him, sisters!" cried Ned. "Be indomitable!"

"Such language," said Mack. "Well, I tell you what. You bring that locket here by daybreak, and you can have your little brother back in one piece. If you don't, you can have him back in lots of pieces. It's up to you."

"But—but—"

"Come along, cully!"

And off he went, sneaking away into the shadows with Ned folded up under his arm.

A pitiful state of affairs!

Just then, a troubling rumble of thunder trundled across the sky. The wisps of fog were whisked aside, and the girls looked up at the stars and saw—

HELP!

The devil?

Well, if he wasn't the devil, then who the devil was he?

Then the figure sprang through the air like a firework, and landed—

Right in front of the girls.
Who **SCREAMED!**

Spring-Heeled Jack blinked. It was as if someone today had said, "Who's Batman?"

Rose and Lily followed as Spring-Heeled Jack led them through a maze of narrow alleys, past crumbling warehouses and sordid opium dens, and on the way they told him their story.

When they'd finished, Spring-Heeled Jack scowled
with anger.

"I'll stop at nothing!" he said. "Your little brother will
be restored, and you shall have your tickets to America. I
know a safe retreat where you can stay. Fear not, for
Spring-Heeled Jack is on the way . . ."

And off they went, at top speed, through the back
streets and the squares and the alleyways, toward a certain pub in Blackfriars.

CHAPTER TWO

"Meanwhile, back at the ranch . . ."
A Western

Meanwhile, back at the orphanage, the Superintendent's assistant had made a horrid discovery.

"Mr. Killjoy!" she said, bursting into the office, where
the Superintendent was doing the accounts. He often did
them late at night, to avoid being overseen.

"What? What? What?" he said, hiding the brandy.

She told him.

"Item: Rose Summers. Item: Lily Summers. Item: Ned
Summers," she said. "Condition: missing, together with
one institutional blanket, one loaf of institutional bread
(last week's quality), and one item of personal property,
to wit, a forbidden locket and chain."

He gaped in horror.

"And when was this discovered?" he said.

"At half-past eight," said Miss Gasket, "when I was
a-going on my rounds, as laid down in my conditions of
service. All the beds I looked in, every blessed one, was

18

full of kids, and all asleep, as per the rules, in the regulation posture, hands by sides and eyes shut. All but three, that is. And there was a window open."

"Do my ears deceive me?" said Mr. Killjoy. "We'll have to get 'em back at once. Ooh, they'll be punished when I gets hold of 'em. Think of Clause 44, Miss Gasket! Think of that, and shiver!"

She did.

Extracts from the Rules and Regulations
Clause 44.

The wages of the guardians shall be paid only while the inmates number the maximum possible, and shall be discontinued if the number falls below that, and shall not be paid until the deficiency is made up.[1]

1. In other words, if they didn't cram in as many kids as the place would hold, they didn't get any wages.

Mr. Killjoy's mighty brain was starting to hum.

"We'll go straight to my friend Sergeant Pincher at the Hangman's Wharf Police Station," he said. "We'll have all the minions of the law combing London for the little perishers. Besides . . ."

Mr. Killjoy locked the accounts away, just in case anyone should come across them by chance and fail to understand them, and then he and his assistant put on their coats and hats and went out to see Sergeant Pincher.

CHAPTER THREE

"What happened next
We'll very soon see . . ."
Janet and Allan Ahlberg, *The Jolly Postman,*
or Other People's Letters

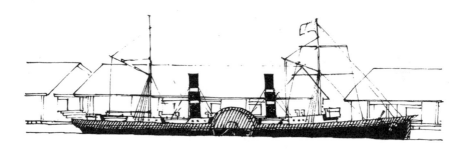

What happened next took place on board the good ship *Indomitable*. She was snug in dock, and all kinds of nautical activities were taking place. Sailors were belaying the taffrail to the bowsprit, boxing the compass, and splicing the binnacle. There was a lot to do before the ship sailed in the morning.

Captain Webster was sitting up in the bridge looking at charts when Jim Bowling, an Able Seaman, came up and saluted.

"Gentleman to see you, sir," he said. "A Mr. Summers."

"Summers," said the Captain. "I know that name . . . Well, show him up, show him up!"

The Captain stowed the charts and turned to face his visitor. And then he remembered Mr. Summers, who'd been a passenger on his ship some time before.

They sat down together and called for grog.

"The last time we met," said the Captain, "you were coming to England on business, if I remember."

"That's right," said Mr. Summers. "It seems a long time ago now. Remarkably fine grog, Andrew."

Mr. Summers's Story

Seven years before, he had gone off to seek his fortune in the Australian gold fields (what an extraordinary coincidence!), and when his ship had sunk, he'd been captured by pirates and forced to toil at an oar with chains around his ankles. When at last he managed to escape, he struggled to raise the cash to come back to England and search for his dear wife and his three little children—Rose, and Lily, and Ned.

WEEP, HOWL.

"No," said Mr. Summers, "I've searched high and low in every part of the country, and found . . . nothing. I can stay in England no longer. I must go abroad, and start a new life in a distant country. Have you room for a passenger?"

"My dear old chap!" said the Captain. "There's always room for you. But you're just in time—we sail with the morning tide."

Jim Bowling saluted smartly and left. The Captain showed Mr. Summers to a comfortable cabin, and the sailors went on reefing the foremast, furling the capstan, and holystoning the futtock shrouds. It was a busy ship.

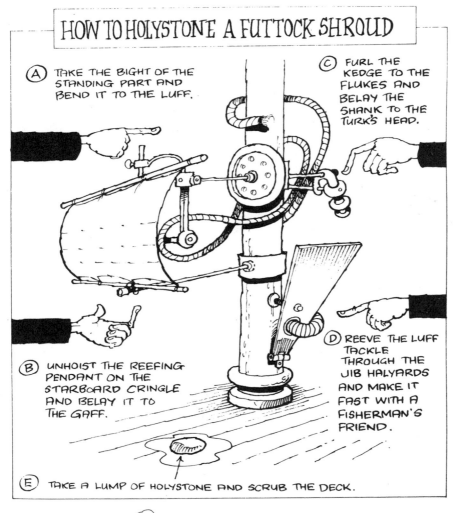

HOW TO HOLYSTONE A FUTTOCK SHROUD

(A) TAKE THE BIGHT OF THE STANDING PART AND BEND IT TO THE LUFF.

(B) UNHOIST THE REEFING PENDANT ON THE STARBOARD CRINGLE AND BELAY IT TO THE GAFF.

(C) FURL THE KEDGE TO THE FLUKES AND BELAY THE SHANK TO THE TURK'S HEAD.

(D) REEVE THE LUFF TACKLE THROUGH THE JIB HALYARDS AND MAKE IT FAST WITH A FISHERMAN'S FRIEND.

(E) TAKE A LUMP OF HOLYSTONE AND SCRUB THE DECK.

I SHOULD HAVE STAYED AT HOME

CHAPTER FOUR

"It was a gloomy old place with high brick walls . . ."
Shirley Hughes, *It's Too Frightening for Me*

In the murkiest, slimiest, darkest corner of the East
End, there was a crumbling old warehouse that even the
rats had deserted. One side of it leaned crazily out over
the river, and the other side leaned gloomily out over the
street.

It was called Turner and Luckett's Medicinal Sarsaparilla Warehouse, but there'd been no sarsaparilla stored
there for years. People believed it was haunted. Mysteri-
ous lights used to gleam behind the broken windows
high up on the top floor, and hideous noises came filter-
ing out over the rooftops in the middle of the night.

It was the headquarters of Mack the Knife and his ap-
palling gang.

When he reached the warehouse, with little Ned still
struggling under his arm, Mack went straight to the top
floor, where a bunch of gangsters were sitting around a
table playing cards by the light of a stolen candle.

Their names were Quinlan, Peregrine, Auberon, and
Filthy.

27

QUINLAN   PEREGRINE   MACK   AUBERON   FILTHY

YOU OUGHT TO SELL THEIR FACES TO A CHEESECAKE FACTORY, TO CURDLE THE MILK. YOU OUGHT TO SELL THEIR FACES TO POSTMEN, TO FRIGHTEN DOGS WITH.

YOU OUGHT TO SELL THEIR FACES TO A TEMPERANCE SOCIETY, TO DISPLAY AS AN EVIL VISION BROUGHT ON BY DRINK!

The gang hadn't met a cheeky victim before, and they didn't like it. They'd have been very nasty indeed to Ned if Mack hadn't stopped them.

"Get back!" he said, beating them off. "The little feller's right, you're the ugliest bunch I've ever seen. Come on, where's that rope?"

Filthy handed him a length of rope. Mack took out his knife to cut through a knot in it.

"Here, go steady, boss," said Filthy. "That rope's got sentimental value for me. They hanged my Uncle Charlie with it last week."

"More fool him for getting caught," said Mack. "Now hold him still while I truss him up."

YOU GREAT BULLIES! YOU UGLY SO-AND-SO'S! YOU GREEDY MURDERING SAUSAGE-FACED PUDDING-HEADED IDLE CONNIVING SCOUNDRELS! YOU FAT-BELLIED STONY-HEARTED SHARK-FACED TIGHT-FISTED SONS OF CRIME! YOU WON'T GET ANYTHING OUT OF THIS, 'CAUSE I'M INDOMITABLE!

"Hark at him, Filthy, what eloquence!" said Mack, when they'd finally gotten him tied up. "If you ever get out of this son, take my advice: become a lawyer. It's the same as thieving, only respectable, and there's no risk of getting caught."

Ned blew a raspberry that shook the window frames.

RUDE RASP!!

WHAT KIND OF A BOOK IS THIS?

"Dear, dear, dear," said Peregrine. "Can't have that. Shall I snite his snitch?"[1]

"Shall I mill his rattlers?"[2] said Auberon.

"Shall I nob him on the canister?"[3] said Quinlan.

"No, no, no," said Mack the Knife. "You know your trouble, boys? You got no craft. You got no imagination. This little feller's going to make us a lot of money. Quinlan, go and steal me some fish and chips. And a bottle of brandy while you're at it."

1. Snite his snitch: give him a good slap in the face.
2. Mill his rattlers: knock his teeth out.
3. Nob him on the canister: whack him on the head.

Now all that time, little Spangle had been faithfully following Ned's scent. It wasn't easy for her, because she was very short, and Mack the Knife had carried Ned in the air for a long way; but finally she reached the sarsaparilla warehouse and squeezed her way through a hole in the wall.

Up the dark stairs she trotted, all in the dark, until she reached the room where the gangsters were tying Ned up.

The moment she saw what they were up to, she sprang in fearlessly.

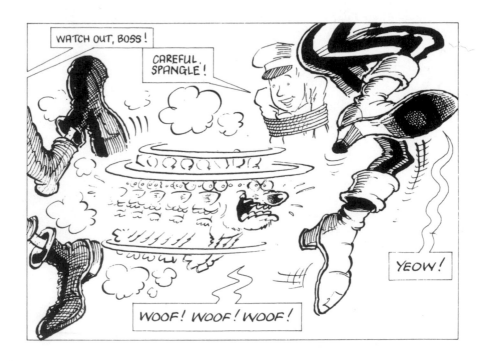

But it was no use. Brave as she was, she just wasn't big enough, and although she managed to nip them all, they very soon had her under control.

"Tut, tut," said Mack. "I can't abide all these harsh feelings. I'm going next door to play me violin. Sling him in the corner—where the spiders are."

So poor Ned was put in the darkest, spideriest corner of the warehouse, and soon the air was filled with hideous howls and screeching sounds as Mack played hymns on his violin.

The gang put their earplugs in and went back to their game of cards.

CHAPTER FIVE

"Underneath the arches . . ."
Flanagan and Allen

Underneath the arches near Blackfriars Bridge, a lonely pieman was wheeling his hot-pie wagon along and whistling to keep his spirits up. There was hardly anyone about that night; he hadn't sold a pie for over an hour.

Then he heard a familiar tune. It was *Santa Lucia,* played on the barrel organ of his friend Antonio Rolipolio.

He turned the corner and saw the organ grinder outside the Rose and Crown, with his monkey Miranda capering about on the barrel organ. But there was no one listening to him. The streets were deserted.

"Poor folks like us have got to take our chance," said the pieman. "Hot pies! Hot pies!"

"Funiculi, funicula," agreed the organ grinder.

Just then, who should come around the corner but the sailor from the *Indomitable,* Able Seaman Jim Bowling. He was glad to be out and about, in spite of the cold, because it gave him the chance to come and say farewell yet again to his sweetheart, Polly Pickles, the barmaid at the Rose and Crown.

He went inside and fetched her out, and they stood beneath the gaslight on the corner of the street to say a tender good-bye.

"Oh, Jim, my beloved, farewell!" she said.

"Farewell, Polly!" he said. "We're off to Baltimore and Panama, and Trebizond and Trinidad and Trincomalee, and Auckland and Shanghai and Wagga Wagga, and it'll be years before I'm back in London. Don't forget me, Polly!"

But it was no good asking Jim to buy anything. His pockets were empty.

"I reckon we're all in the same fix, mates," he said. "Still, Polly, I'll pick up a shilling or two tonight, 'cause there's a gent on board who wants his case picked up before we sail. I daresay he'll slip me a bit of money, if I gets it to him smartish. So I'm off now, Polly, love, and the first stop on the way to Baltimore is the Saveloy Hotel!"

"Oh, sweetheart!" said Polly. "Take care!"

"I will!"

"And come back safe!"

"I will!"

"And don't forget your little Polly!"

"As if I ever could!"

The pieman and the organ grinder, not to mention the monkey, were overcome at the sight of such devotion.

And so Jim left, leaving Polly weeping under the gas-light.

"Well, there's no money for us here, mate," said the pieman. "Time to move on. Hot pies! Hot pies!"

And he trundled his pie wagon away. The organ grinder sat his monkey back on the organ and began to pack up too.

"Come along, monkey," he said. "Good-a night, pretty Polly. Love will-a find a way!"

"Good night, Signor Rolipolio," said Polly. "Good night, monkey . . ."

Oh, well, thought Polly. Someday my Jim will come back, and then we'll be as happy as fleas on a nice warm dog.

She was just about to go back into the pub when—

Polly knew Spring-Heeled Jack well. He'd saved her from some robbers only a month or two before, so she wasn't afraid of him at all. And when she heard what he had to say, she was glad to help.

"Ooh, that's awful!" she said, when they told her about Mack the Knife and Ned and the locket and everything. "But you come inside—you'll be safe here. You can rely on Jack. If anyone can save your little brother, he can!"

FEAR NOT! I SHALL RETURN.
SPRING-HEELED JACK IS ON THE TRAIL!

And he leapt away over the rooftops with incredible speed, making a whizzing noise like a firework and leaving a trail of smoke in the air.

"Oh, miss," said Rose, "we're in such trouble!"

"We must get Ned back, you see," said Lily, "and then get to the Docks in time, and . . ."

"There, there," said Polly. "You come on in. I'll see if I can find you a sandwich. You look as if you could do with a feed."

So in they went, and the cold, foggy street was empty again.

But not for long.

Because an odd, bedraggled little creature like a mournful moth, or like a secondhand angel, was flapping dismally through the foggy air, invisible to everyone except us. It flew in and hovered near the window of the pub, as if it was waiting for someone.

And a second later, that someone arrived. It was Filthy.

Filthy was ambitious. Besides, he didn't much like what Mack the Knife was up to. He thought there'd be openings for a smart young man, and he'd spotted something going on a minute ago outside the Rose and Crown—something he could turn to his advantage.

So he crept up to the window—and the little shabby mothlike thing came and sat on his shoulder.

That was how they dealt with consciences in London. The other members of the gang had no consciences at all, or else they'd gotten rid of them better than Filthy had. With an uneasy look behind him, Filthy went into the Rose and Crown.

CHAPTER SIX

"There is an air of cold, solitary desolation
about the noiseless streets . . ."
Charles Dickens, *Sketches by Boz*

There was an air of cold, solitary desolation about the noiseless streets. Mr. Killjoy and Miss Gasket had been combing them for hours, and Sergeant Pincher from the Hangman's Wharf Police Station had got his best men searching too. There was hardly a corner of London they didn't poke their noses into. They were only bothering because of the locket, of course.

And not long after Rose and Lily arrived at the Rose and Crown, and only a minute or two after Filthy did, Mr. Killjoy and Miss Gasket did too.

They were feeling chilly, and Mr. Killjoy was thinking that he'd like to slip into the saloon bar for a large brandy. It wouldn't be fitting for a lady to be seen in a public house, so he'd send out a glass of lemonade for Miss Gasket while she kept watch on the pavement.

He was just explaining this to her when he felt a tap on his shoulder.

Filthy looked around nervously in case his conscience was watching, but he couldn't see it, so he went on:

"I thought as how I heard the lady here address you as Mr. Killjoy, and I thought to myself, I thought, I wonder if this man could be the Mr. Albert Killjoy as runs the Alderman Cawn-Plaster Memorial Orphanage?"

"That person has the honor of being me," said Mr. Killjoy austerely. "Well, my man, what is it? What is it?"

"Get off," muttered Filthy, brushing something off his shoulder. "I beg your pardon, sir. The thing is—I knows the whereabouts of a certain pair of little girls."

"Oh," said Mr. Killjoy. "Ah."

Then Miss Gasket took him aside.

Mr. Killjoy was a soft touch, but Miss Gasket was terrifying. Filthy nearly quailed as she glared at him.

"I suppose you intend to ask a price for this information?" she said.

"Well," said Filthy, "I thought maybe a payment of five guineas would cover it. Sort of an honorarium kind of thing."

"A dishonorarium, more like," said Miss Gasket. "I'll give you *one,* and that's your lot."

Mr. Killjoy was deeply impressed, but Filthy wasn't.

"One guinea?" he said, shocked. "One guinea, after all I've done? If you said four, now . . ."

"If I agreed to four, I'd be a fool," said Miss Gasket. "Two at the most."

"Make it three?" said Filthy humbly.

"Certainly not," she said. "Two, and that's your lot."

Mr. Killjoy handed Filthy two guineas. Filthy stowed them inside his pocket quickly before his conscience saw how much he'd gotten.

So Filthy slunk away. But around the corner—

OH NO! NOT YOU AGAIN! I SHALL HAVE A ROTTEN NIGHT, AND NO MISTAKE...

Inside the Rose and Crown, Mr. Killjoy was demanding to see Polly Pickles.

"She's in the public bar," said the landlord, "doing her job, what she's paid for. She's spent enough time this evening canoodling with her sweetheart."

"Don't argue with me," said Mr. Killjoy. "Have you a private parlor, my man?"

"Yes, I have, and it costs a guinea to hire it," said the landlord.

Mr. Killjoy drew himself up to his full height, and then handed over a guinea.

"Be good enough to show us in there," he said. "And subsequently have this Pickles person brought before us, or else face the full rigor of the law."

The landlord said something rude, which Miss Gasket didn't quite catch, and then went to fetch Polly.

"We'll have to play this careful," said Mr. Killjoy to Miss Gasket as they went into the parlor. "We don't want 'em to take fright and skedaddle."

So when Polly came in a minute later, they were all smiles and sweetness.

43

"Now, Miss Pickles," said Miss Gasket, "three of our little charges has gone astray. Our *dear* little charges. And naturally we're upset and concerned—"

"And we've come searching for them," said Mr. Killjoy, "sparing no expense of time or money—"

"Just so's we get our little darlings back!" said Miss Gasket.

"Well, I don't know," said Polly. "They did say they came from the Alderman Cawn-Plaster Memorial Orphanage, not the Happy Smiles whatever-it-was . . ."

"The little monkeys!" said Mr. Killjoy fondly. "Always ready for a joke, them kids. We've laughed together many a time, haven't we, Miss Gasket?"

"Oh, those jolly evenings in the Home," she said, "with the little darlings around our feet, playing their merry tricks!"

Polly wasn't used to dealing with important people, and these two seemed very important. And she wasn't used to dealing with crafty deceptive sneaks either. These two were worse than weasels, but she didn't know that they were lying.

"Well," she said, "I'm not sure . . ."

"There," said Miss Gasket. "You're anxious about their safety, I can tell."

"Yes, I am," said Polly. "They're ever so upset, the pair of them, and worn out too."

"Ahh," said Miss Gasket fondly.

"You fetch 'em here, Miss Pickles," said Mr. Killjoy. "Take it from me, they'll be overjoyed to come home again. They'll be frantic with glee."

"Well, if you say so, sir," said Polly, "I'll have to believe you, you being in your position and me being in mine, and the world being what it is. All right, I'll fetch 'em out."

And out she went, and a short while later she came back with the girls.

And before they could get away, Mr. Killjoy had seized Lily in his great red hands. But Rose was too quick for Miss Gasket; she dodged out of the room and down the corridor as quick as a cat.

"Stop! Stop, you hussy!" cried Miss Gasket. "Come back here!"

"Run, Rose, quick!" shouted Polly. "Go to the Saveloy Hotel—ask for Jim Bowling! He'll help you!"

And Rose was gone.

Without another word, Mr. Killjoy and Miss Gasket swept out, dragging poor Lily behind them.

"Oh, Lily, I'm sorry!" Polly cried, and she tried to hold on to Lily's hand, but Mr. Killjoy and Miss Gasket were too strong for her. She ran to the door after them, only to see them disappear around the corner, with Lily still calling Mr. Killjoy every name Polly had ever heard of, and several she hadn't.

"Oh, what a fool I am!" she said to herself. "How could I let meself be taken in like that? Them poor kids, and they was relying on me, and I handed 'em over just like that . . ."

Poor Polly. It wasn't her fault, but she felt it was, and that was bad enough. Saying good-bye to Jim, and then this . . . It was too much. She howled and howled.

And meanwhile Rose was running full tilt through the dark streets, looking for the Saveloy Hotel . . .

CHAPTER SEVEN

"I didn't dare stop to rest . . ."
Tove Jansson, *The Exploits of Moominpappa*

Rose didn't dare stop to rest. She ran like the wind, up alleyways, across busy squares, down desolate streets. She couldn't afford to be afraid of what might be hiding around dark corners. From the Rose and Crown she ran full tilt until she came to the Strand, and then she stopped and looked up and down.

The gaslights shone down on hansom cabs and carriages, on gentlemen in top hats and flower girls in rags. There were theaters and restaurants and embassies and clubs, and the biggest, poshest, swankiest place of all was the Saveloy Hotel.

SAVELOY HOTEL
MENU

Le clear soup
Le thick soup
Le soup avec bits in
Le soup de turtle

Le fish avec beaucoup de bones
Le fish avec no bones
Le sauce pour le fish
Le waiter pour le sauce over le fish

Le roast boeuf
La vache entière en croûte à la Desperate Dan*
Le roast mouton avec le sauce de mint
Les saucissons dans une montagne de pommes de terre mashés
Le suprême de volaille à la rencontre du King of Brazil avec
sa Petite Amie du Moment

Les végétables
Les chips
Les beans bakes

Le green salade
Le salade de tous les autres couleurs

Le dick spotte
Le jelly
Le blancmange
L'ice cream
Les pancakes

Les sardines sur toast
Les eggs scramblés

Le coffee
Le brandy
Les cigars
Le Turkish Delight

*Cow Pie

CHIEF - BOWER -
AND - SCRAPER

RECEPTION - DESK -
POINTER - OUTER

STAIRCASE - POINTER -
OUTER - AND - PORTER -
SUMMONER

49

When Rose got to the hotel entrance and looked in at all those servants and guests, her heart sank. How was she going to get past all that poshness, dressed in rags as she was?

However, there was always the back door. She might be able to get in and find Jim Bowling that way. The trouble was, she didn't even know who Jim Bowling was, or what he looked like, or anything. Still, he was her only hope, so she slipped down the courtyard beside the hotel and looked for the back way in.

Meanwhile, in the great kitchen, twenty sauce cooks and thirty meat cooks and forty vegetable cooks and fifty pastry cooks were preparing a banquet for the King of Brazil and all the other guests. The chief cook was shouting at them all, and the cooks were shouting at the waiters, and the waiters were shouting at each other, and the air was full of delicious smells and ferocious heat.

PAGEBOY-CALLER-AND-SENDER-ON-ERRANDS

PORTER

PAGEBOY (WATCH OUT FOR HIM IN A PAGE OR TWO)

In the middle of all the noise and rush, Jim Bowling was making his way out with Mr. Summers's suitcase. Since he was only a common sailor, they couldn't possibly let him go out through the front door. But Jim didn't mind, because he suddenly spotted an old friend.

"Casey Wilkins!" he said. "Shiver me timbers and blow me down, but wherever I go, Shanghai or San Francisco or Bombay, I'm sure to find some old shipmate ashore, snug in a cushy berth and good for a glass of grog. How are you, Casey?"

Casey Wilkins was long, lean, and miserable. He'd been a ship's carpenter when Jim had sailed with him. He was a pastry cook now, and he was kneading some pastry for some *viande de saucisses en croûte à la graisse froide.*[1]

"Hello, Jim," he said. "Keep you voice down. See that fat cook? The bloke in charge? He's worse than any bo-sun you've ever sailed with, mate. Wherever you go, there's blokes whose only job is bossing the likes of you and me around."

1. Sausage rolls.

"Still the same old cheerful spirit," said Jim. "What's the rush for? Is it extra busy tonight?"

"We've got the King of Brazil in," said Casey. "He likes his food, King Alfonso does."

"Oh, the King of Brazil, eh," said Jim. "Posh."

The fat cook came past with a saucepan, and Jim couldn't resist.

At that moment the door at the far end of the kitchen opened and Rose looked through. No one noticed her in all the hubbub, but she spotted Jim at once, because he was the only person in the place not dressed like a cook.

And Rose was just about to do that when someone else ran up. This time it was a pageboy. The place was definitely getting crowded.

It's all kicks and no ha'pence, being a pageboy.

Casey Wilkins led Jim and Rose up the servants' staircase and along lots of narrow corridors and then up some more stairs into an attic.

"What do we do?" said Jim, who was getting nervous already.

"Nothing to it," said Casey. "Just squeeze out through the skylight and there you are, mate. It's a bit steep and slippery, mind—just hang on to the chimneys and you'll be all right . . ."

He had to leave them then and go back and make some more pastry.

Jim squeezed out first with the suitcase and Rose came after him, listening carefully all the time for Miss Gasket and the policeman. They wobbled their way along the roof, clinging tightly to the chimneys. Rose had to tell Jim where to put his feet, because he had his eyes shut.

Meanwhile, Miss Gasket had gone through all the rooms in the hotel like a simoom.[2] The policeman trailed nervously behind her, apologizing. He was called P. C. Tweedle. He wasn't much good at chasing people; what he liked best was helping them across the road. He'd never met anyone as fierce as Miss Gasket before, and he wasn't sure how fierce she wanted him to be.

"Er—excuse me, miss—" he said, as she came charging out of a linen cupboard like a khamsin.[3]

"No, they're not in there," she said. "Come on. We'll do the attics next. Wake up, man! Move yourself!"

And off she went like a harmattan.[4] Gulping, he followed her up the stairs.

2. A hot wind.
3. A hot wind.
4. A hot wind.

Of course, they found nothing in the attics except beetles and woodworms, and it wasn't long before Miss Gasket saw the skylight. It was still open, because Rose hadn't managed to shut it from outside, and Jim couldn't have shut it anyway with his eyes closed.

With a snort of derision, Miss Gasket told P. C. Tweedle to kneel down. She stood on his shoulders and hauled herself through the skylight, and then pulled him up after her. He didn't like it at all.

And at the other end of the roof . . .

P. C. Tweedle was horrified. He didn't like heights any more than Jim did.

"He looks dangerous to me," he said. "He's a desperate character, miss. He's probably got knives and guns and dynamite in that suitcase. I think we'd better call for reinforcements—"

Miss Gasket hit him.

"Ow!" he said. "All right, all right—I'll arrest him."

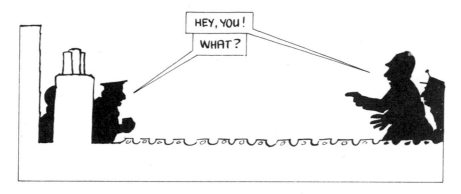

"He says he ain't, miss," said P. C. Tweedle. "Perhaps we'd better—"

Then he saw the look in Miss Gasket's eye, and ducked. Her handbag went whistling past his head.

"You're a lily-livered poltroon," she told him. "You're a disgrace to your noble helmet. I'll have to go and get him myself!"

Jim certainly didn't want to fall off, but he certainly didn't want any more of Miss Gasket.

"Hang on there, Rose!" he shouted. "I'll go and deal with the chicken-faced copper over there, and then I'll come back and sort the old girl out. I won't be a minute."

"Now, now," said P. C. Tweedle, dodging behind a chimney. "I strongly advise you to stand back."

"Too late for that, mate," said Jim. "I'm getting cross now. Come out here!"

"Now, steady on, steady on," said P. C. Tweedle, darting around one side of the chimney while Jim came around the other. "What I advise you to do is to count to ten to improve your temper."

"Keep still!" shouted Jim. "Stop dodging about like a cuckoo in a clock!"

"I don't want to get my uniform creased, you see—"

"Uniform my foot," said Jim. "I know what I can do with you. Come here!"

"No, no, no—"

But when he turned around there was no sign at all of Rose or Miss Gasket. Apart from the constable's legs, the roof was bare.

So he took the suitcase and clambered back through the skylight, ran down the stairs, and shot out of the Saveloy Hotel like a sirocco.[5] None of the servants knew what hit them.

5. Yes, you guessed it.

CHAPTER EIGHT

"So this was how things stood . . ."
Sergei Sergeyevich Prokofiev, *Peter and the Wolf*

So this was how things stood: Lily was caught, and Rose was caught, and Ned was tied up in the dark, and poor little Spangle had been defenestrated. The gangsters had had their cocoa and cookies and gone to bed early, all except for Filthy, who was still walking around trying to lose his conscience. Mack the Knife had been playing his violin for hours. Every so often he'd stop and sharpen his knife in a meaningful kind of way, and smoke a horrible cigar. Ned wasn't sure which was worst: the cigar, or the knife sharpening, or the violin playing—or wondering whether Spangle was all right.

Everything was about as bad as it could be, thought Ned.

He wished the girls would come and bring the locket so that Mack would let him go. If they did, they wouldn't be able to run away properly, though; they'd all have to go begging around the streets, and they'd probably get sent back to the Alderman Cawn-Plaster Memorial Orphanage.

So part of him hoped they wouldn't bring the locket to Mack but that they'd go and sail away to America as they'd planned, so that at least two of them would be safe and free. He felt very noble when he thought that. He imagined the girls in their prosperous new home in New York or San Francisco, looking sadly at an empty picture frame draped in black. There'd have been a picture of him if they'd had one, but they didn't, of course, so it would have to be empty. Perhaps they could have little curtains hung across it, and a brass plate saying:

IN MEMORY OF OUR BROTHER NED,
WHOSE NOBLE AND FEARLESS NATURE
DID NOT SHRINK FROM THE FINAL SACRIFICE

He thought about that for a good long while, for at least a minute and a half, and decided that there'd probably hardly been anyone as noble as he was, ever. He wished he were a bit more fearless, though. And he wished Spangle would find her way back. She was fearless enough for both of them.

And then once more he heard sharpening sounds from the next room, and the door opened, and there stood Mack . . .

Just then, Ned caught sight of something even more horrible than Mack the Knife.

Crouching up on a high window ledge, with his eyes glowing and his whiskers bristling and his tail swishing, and with a wisp of sulfurous smoke drifting down from him, sat—

"The devil!" said Ned. "He's come to get you, look!"

Mack laughed. "No such thing, cocky," he said. "And I should know. I'm the most evil man in the world, and I tell you straight, there ain't no devil, there ain't no hell, there ain't no nothing. Except this place, which is bad enough. Now come on—it won't take half a minute."

"I can see him!" Ned shouted. "He's up there—his horns, his claws, his tail—he's crouching on the window sill—he's going to get you! He will, he will!"

"Oh, no, he won't," said Mack, coming closer.

"Oh, yes, he will!"

"Oh, no, he won't. I know quite well there's nothing on that window sill, because nothing could climb the warehouse wall. For the last time, there's nothing there!"

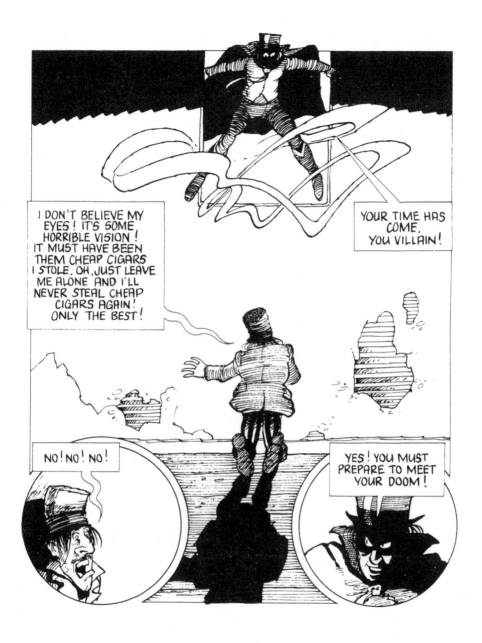

That wasn't what Mack had in mind at all.

And as Spring-Heeled Jack came closer and closer, with the hideous glare in his eyes getting fiercer and fiercer, with his whiskers whiskering bristlier and bristlier, Mack sank to his knees.

"Don't take me!" he begged. "You don't want me—I'm horrible and evil. Take this young lad here—he's got a nice, pure, innocent soul, sweet as a nut!"

"I don't want him," said Spring-Heeled Jack, coming closer. "I want *you,* and I want you now."

"Oh, blimey," said Mack faintly. "Look—what about a bet? Eh?"

"A bet?" said Spring-Heeled Jack, twisting his whiskers.

But there was an interested gleam in his eye, and Mack went on:

"Yes! A contest of evil! I'll tell you the most evil thing I can think of, and you tell me the most evil thing you can think of, and we'll see which is the worst. And the one who thinks of that—wins!"

"Hmm," said Spring-Heeled Jack. "I like it. I think I'll take you on."

Mack felt a shudder of relief. He'd thought of so many evil things in his life that he reckoned he was bound to win. He rubbed his hands together—but then Spring-Heeled Jack shook his head.

WAIT! NOT IN HERE. WE DON'T WANT TO BLEMISH THESE INNOCENT EARS WITH OUR TALES OF EVIL.

THANK YOU VERY MUCH, I'M SURE...

COME NEXT DOOR THEN. I'VE GOT A NICE ROOM THERE—
IT OVERLOOKS THE RIVER. HA HA HA !
SEE YOU IN A MINUTE, CULLY . . .

And off they went, leaving little Ned once more in the dark.

Horrible, creepy thoughts crawled all over each other in his mind. He didn't know which would be worse—to be left with Mack, or to be left with the devil. And even if they both vanished, there was still the rest of the gang.

But just as he was feeling completely abandoned, there was an excited little yap in the darkness nearby, and a cold nose snuffled against his neck, and a hot tongue licked eagerly at his cheeks.

"Spangle!" he whispered. "You're all right! Thank goodness! No—take your tongue out of my nose—stop it—keep quiet—that's a good girl—shhh!"

Spangle was so happy to have found Ned again that she did exactly what he said, even though she couldn't understand it. And as for Ned, he was so happy to have her with him that he felt like licking *her*. She lay right up close beside him, and they listened as hard as they could.

Then they heard a whispering from next door, like rats' feet pattering over bones.

Silence . . . And then a cry of *"Oh no! What a tale of evil! Wicked, wicked!"*

But whose voice was it?

Ned couldn't tell.

And then came more whispering, like the sound of a ghost brushing its long-dead hair in a dusty mirror.

Silence. Then—

"No, no, no! I can't bear it! It's too evil for words! I'm done for . . . Horrible, horrible, horrible!"

But whose voice was it?

Ned still couldn't tell. And then there came a lifeless thump as someone fell to the floor . . . And then a slow, dragging noise . . . And then, after a long time, a far-distant splash in the river below.

Gulp, thought Ned. Spangle's hair bristled all over, and she gave a tiny howl. She couldn't help it.

Then came a creak as the door opened, and a long shadow fell across the floor . . .

CHAPTER NINE

"AAAAARRGGGHHH!"
David Mostyn, *The Beano*

"**W**ell?" said Ned shakily. "Who won?"

Slow footsteps came creaking toward him over the dusty floorboards. Spangle's nose was trembling against his neck, and his eyes were shut tight, and there was a horrible silence.

Then Ned felt hands on his shoulders, lifting him gently up.

"Well done, Ned," said the voice of the devil.

Ned felt him undoing the rope, and opened his eyes. And then he saw that it couldn't be the devil, because Spangle was licking him furiously, so he must be all right.

Pausing only to tie the other gangsters (who were fast asleep) firmly into their beds so they wouldn't be able to get out till the police came, Jack and Ned and Spangle went down the rickety old stairs and out onto the dark wharf.

But while Jack was untying a convenient rowboat . . .

Whatever it was that Spring-Heeled Jack had told him, it hadn't been enough to finish Mack off. His leathery old soul had been scorched a bit, but the water must have cooled him down, because he came crawling out as evil as ever and thirsting for revenge.

And he nearly had it, too.

But Spangle saved the day. She made straight for him as if she'd been shot from a catapult. Her little teeth were snapping, and her little paws were scratching, and the growl that came out of her throat would have done credit to a werewolf.

"So you didn't need me after all?" said Spring-Heeled
Jack, when Ned and Spangle had finished. "Just sit on
him for a minute and we'll tie him up."

And taking a rope from the boat, he leapt into the air
on his spring-heeled boots and passed the end through a
pulley at the very top of the warehouse.

"He can stay there till the police come and take him down," said Jack as they rowed up the river. "It's a nice view from up there. He'll enjoy it if he stops wriggling."

CHAPTER TEN

"You mustn't cry, my dear . . ."
Russell Hoban, *The Mouse and His Child*

Polly was ever so miserable. She was so unhappy that the landlord of the Rose and Crown stopped her from serving in the bar and made her go and do the washing up instead. Tears in the dishwater didn't matter, but tears in the beer made it taste funny, and the customers complained.

She was longing for Jim to come back so she could have a really good howl. But he wasn't due back for about two years, and thinking of that made her cry even more, and she had to empty the tears out of the bowl and put some fresh water in.

So when she looked up and saw Jim's face at the scullery window, she gave a yelp of surprise.

He told Polly what had happened, and they sat down by the kitchen fire, feeling miserable.

"I reckon we've let 'em both down, Polly," said Jim. "Poor little kids. D'you know what?"

"What?"

"I don't reckon they ought to get away with it, them Superintendents. I reckon someone ought to put a stop to it."

"But you ought to be getting back to your ship, Jim! And you got that gentleman's suitcase to take, and all . . ."

"I don't care about that, Poll. This is a matter of a sailor's honor!"

He looked so noble sitting there, with his fists on his knees and his jaw clenched, that he might have been the sailor William in the play *Black-Ey'd Susan,* about to be hanged from the yardarm.

"Oh, Jim," she said.

And she might easily have kissed him or something, except that he suddenly stopped looking noble and looked excited instead.

"Here, Poll," he said, "I've just had a brain wave!"

"Supposing them guardians thought the kids' ma and pa had turned up—they'd have to let 'em go, wouldn't they?"

"Well, I suppose they would, Jim, but—what are you doing?"

Jim had flung open the suitcase and was rummaging around among the clothes. He found a suit and held it up against himself.

"There," he said. "We could pretend to be them, couldn't we? How's that?"

Polly didn't know what to say. So she dried her eyes and kissed him.

"Oh, Jim!" she said, having found some words. "All right, we'll do it!"

So they disguised themselves, and set out for the Alderman Cawn-Plaster Memorial Orphanage.

And only a minute or two later by the kitchen clock, the cat suddenly sat up.

Spring-Heeled Jack usually came to the scullery door when he visited Polly, because if he'd come in through the front door, none of the customers would ever have gone there again.

But Polly wasn't there, and nor were the girls. Ned was so tired that he sat down with Spangle and went to sleep, while Spring-Heeled Jack crept through the whole house and found no one.

Something was wrong. It wasn't like Polly to vanish like that. Jack went back to the kitchen, where Ned was nearly fast asleep, and there he spotted the suitcase.

I WONDER.

EDWARD MONTGOMERY SUMMERS

NED, WHAT'S YOUR FULL NAME?

MMM? WOSSAT? EDWARD MONTGOMERY SUMMERS, JUST LIKE MY FATHER WAS.

HIGH TIDE IN FIFTY MINUTES - THERE'S NO TIME TO WASTE! COME ON!

EH? WHAT? WHERE ARE WE GOING?

I'LL TELL YOU ON THE WAY! JUST HOLD ON TIGHT!

WHAT WITH DEVILS AND DOGS, THIS PLACE IS GOING TO THE DOGS, OR THE DEVIL...

DEAD EXCITING THOUGH!

CHAPTER ELEVEN

"Meanwhile, back at the orphanage . . ."
Philip Pullman, *Spring-Heeled Jack*

Meanwhile, back at the orphanage, Mr. Killjoy and Miss Gasket were congratulating themselves.

They sat in Mr. Killjoy's office eating cheese-and-pickle sandwiches and drinking sarsaparilla cordial. Mr. Killjoy had put some brandy in his, because he found it helped his digestion.

He was just about to look at it when there was a ring from the doorbell.

Mr. Killjoy jumped, and stuffed the locket into his waistcoat.

"Who can that be?" he whispered.

"Oh, bless my soul, it's the police—it's that man that got stuffed down the chimney—"

"Not your responsibility, Miss Gasket—deny everything!"

The bell rang again, louder.

"Come on, open up!" came a voice from outside. "We know you're in there!"

"Better go and let them in, Miss Gasket," said Mr. Killjoy hurriedly.

She scuttled out. He took a quick swig of brandy and made sure the account books were out of sight, just in case the visitors should be troubled by trying to work out what some of the entries meant.

A moment later, Miss Gasket showed Jim and Polly in.

Polly had rouged and powdered her face, and she was wearing a very grand dress that the landlord's missus had worn to the Gas Fitters' Ball. She hadn't told the landlord's missus, and there'd be ructions later, but this was an emergency. Jim was wearing one of Mr. Summers's suits. He'd stuck on a great big false pair of whiskers as well, but he wasn't at all sure of them.

Mr. Killjoy began to swell up and go red, so Polly thought she'd better step in.

"Please, sir," she said, "you'll have to forgive me dear husband, him having gone through torments in the Australian gold fields, 'cause he's a bit upset, as I am meself. You see, we've heard that our dear little children, what we believed was lost, is in your care!"

"We'll have to see about that," said Miss Gasket tightly.

"Too right you will," said Jim.

"Now, now, dear," said Polly. Then she announced: "Our names is Mr. and Mrs. Summers, and our kiddies' names is Lily, Rose, and Ned."

Well, that took Mr. Killjoy by surprise.

She had a gleam in her eye. To Mr. Killjoy's astonishment, she turned back to Polly and said, "Very well, Mrs. Summers, dear. You shall have them."

She left the room. They all watched her go, and then turned back to each other.

There was a very awkward silence indeed. Jim was looking suspiciously at Mr. Killjoy, and Mr. Killjoy was looking suspiciously at Jim, and Polly was trying to look innocent.

"Very seasonable weather we're having," she said brightly.

No one said a word.

"Very seasonable for the time of year, I mean," she said.

And then the door opened, and there was a double gasp.

Miss Gasket seemed to be enjoying herself, and nobody could work out why. Then she sprang a surprise.

"Before we can release the dear little ones into your care," she said sweetly, "there's the Orphanage Regulations to be complied with."

"Oh, yes?" said Jim. "I don't see any need for that."

"Just a little check," said Miss Gasket, "to make sure no one's impersonating anyone they ain't."

Polly gulped. But there was no way around that, and she and Jim had to take the pieces of paper and the pencils Miss Gasket handed out. She gave some to Rose and Lily too, and they all waited nervously for what Miss Gasket would say next.

"Now then," she said. "It's very simple. You can all write down the answers to three questions. And if your answers match up with the girls' ones, why, you can take them away!"

"It's no good, sweetheart," Jim whispered, "I reckon we'll just have to give way to despair!"

"Question number one," said Miss Gasket, smiling like a crocodile. "What was the name of the little cottage where you all lived before you was so sadly split up?"

"Oh! Oh!" said Polly. "I think I'm going to faint!"

And she pressed the back of her hand to her head and sank to the floor with a graceful thump.

As soon as he'd written it down, he rushed over to Polly. But he knew she was only pretending, and it had given him an idea about what to do next.

"There, there, me love," he said. "All right now?"

"Oh, I don't know what came over me," said Polly, heaving herself delicately up. "There, I'm quite restored."

"Oh, good," said Miss Gasket. "And now for the second question: what's the date of Lily's birthday?"

That was a tricky one. But it only took Jim a second to think of a way around it.

So far so good. Polly scribbled the answer down, and then rushed to the window with the others.

"Where? Where is it?" she said.

"It's gone now," said Jim. "You missed it. What a shame."

They all stood away from the window. Mr. Killjoy had got a bit bumped in the rush, mainly by Jim, and he wasn't very happy about it.

But Miss Gasket was impatient to get on. Jim was wondering what Polly would think of this time, and wondering whether he ought to think of something in case she couldn't, and wondering how they'd manage if neither of them did; but mainly, he was bothered by a stray bit of whisker that was sticking up his nose.

"And now we come to the third question," said Miss Gasket. "What was—"

But finally he realized.

"Oh, that's the end, then," he said bitterly. "But I tell you this—I think it's a blooming disgrace!"

"That's the first true thing you've said tonight, young man," said Mr. Killjoy. "Miss Gasket, go and fetch Sergeant Pincher from the police station!"

"With the greatest of pleasure," said Miss Gasket, and she went out into the hall to put on her galoshes, her fox-fur tippet, and her hat with the left-hand half of a tropical bird stuck to it.

She was too stingy to take a candle with her, and she knew where everything was without looking, or so she thought. So she had the shock of her life when she reached for the door handle and found—a hand!

It was a hard, cold hand, and it gripped hers with iron strength. You should have heard her scream! It made plaster fall from the ceiling (what little there was of it) and it woke all the children in the orphanage.

They came crowding out of their cold beds and peered down the chilly stairs, and the sight that met their eyes was enough to curdle water.

For there in the light of the lamp held in Mr. Killjoy's horrified hand, as he opened the door of the office, was—

As for Mr. Killjoy, he couldn't believe his eyes. He'd had either too much brandy or too little, and he couldn't decide which.

But then the frightful vision spoke, in tones of thunder.

"I am Spring-Heeled Jack," he said. "And I want to have words with you."

And in came Spangle like a rocket. She knew Spring-Heeled Jack now, so she didn't waste any sniffs on him, but there were enough strange smells in the orphanage to keep her happy for hours. She didn't fancy Mr. Killjoy's smell very much, so she just gave his ankle a nip and then bounded up the stairs to smell all the kids. They were delighted.

Mr. Killjoy and Miss Gasket could tell they weren't wanted down there, and they were about to sneak upstairs and beat a few of the children to relieve their feelings, when Spring-Heeled Jack put out a clawlike hand and stopped them.

And Mr. Killjoy went scuttling into the office after them to make certain Mr. Hawkshaw heard about some of the things Miss Gasket had done wrong.

"Spring-Heeled Jack?" said Rose. "What's going to happen to us now? Can we get on that ship and go to America?"

"Yes," he said. "And, in fact, I've got a surprise for you. But we'll have to hurry. Ned! Lily!"

But Rose had something important to say first.

"Please," she said, plucking at his sleeve. "It's all the others. It don't seem fair somehow, but I know they can't all come with us, only I would like 'em to be a bit better off than what they are . . ."

Spring-Heeled Jack looked up the dark stairs. The landing was crowded with faces, silent and wide-eyed in the gloom.

And among them was Spangle. She was as quiet as all the rest, and every so often looked up and licked the nearest dirty face. Ned could tell what she wanted from the way she was looking at him, and he could tell what all the kids wanted, too.

So he said "Spring-Heeled Jack? You know Spangle? Well, she—well, I mean—could you—I mean, they don't let 'em have pets here, but maybe—and she'd probably fall off the ship anyway—and—could they keep her here?"

Leaving Spangle was even more difficult than facing up to Mack the Knife. But after all, he and Rose and Lily were going to be free now, and none of the others were. And Spangle would certainly look after them well.

"I understand," said Spring-Heeled Jack. "Well, I don't think Mr. Killjoy or Miss Gasket will be here for very long, and there's bound to be a change in the rules about pets and things. The new Superintendent will see to that."

"Who's that going to be?" said Rose.

"And what's going to happen to Polly?" said Lily. "She'll lose her job when the landlord's missus finds out about the dress . . ."

"If you put two and two together," said Spring-Heeled Jack, "you'll come up with the answer. Leave it all to me. And now we must hurry. We've got to get to the Docks before Jim's ship sails."

"Oh, yes," said Jim. "That gentleman'll be wanting his suitcase."

"It's more important than that," said Spring-Heeled Jack. "That gentleman is—the children's father!"

"Yes," said Spring-Heeled Jack, "the name on the suit-case is Edward Montgomery Summers, and if he isn't your father, I'm a cucumber. Come on—I've got a cab waiting—but we'll have to be quick!"

Ned shot up the stairs and said good-bye to Spangle, and the girls said good-bye to Polly and all the kids.

"Oh—quick—" said Rose, fumbling for the locket. "We won't need this now—I'll take the picture out—and then can you sell it and give the money to the orphanage so the kids can have some decent blankets?"

"Yes," said Spring-Heeled Jack. "But *hurry*."

There was just time for a tender farewell.

CHAPTER TWELVE

"We haven't a moment to lose, Captain . . ."
Hergé, *The Adventures of Tintin: The Shooting Star*

Th=[]hey hadn't a moment to lose. The terrified cabdriver hung on with both hands as Spring-Heeled Jack took the reins and cracked the whip and set the horse galloping through the empty streets toward the Docks, with the children holding tight inside and Jim (and the suitcase) clinging on behind.

Already the sky was lighter in the east, and the tide was plucking and knocking at the ships in the dock. The Captain was about to give orders for the gangplank to be raised. A fat little tug was puffing and snorting nearby.

In his cabin, Mr. Summers was fast asleep, dreaming of his lost children. Into his sleep came the distant sounds of the sailors reefing the binnacle and close-hauling the anchor chain, and the distant smells of breakfast from the galley.

"Not long now," he murmured.

The sailors on the tug threw a stout rope up to the sailors on the *Indomitable,* and they tied it tightly to a solid bit of ship. The Captain watched to make sure they didn't use a granny knot.

Meanwhile, Spring-Heeled Jack was driving like a demon. The cab was hurtling through the streets, swaying around corners, rattling over cobblestones, and shaking the children about like nobody's business.

They'd just lurched around a corner into the West India Dock Road when—

Spread out all over the road were a ton and a half of Brussels sprouts. A wagon belonging to the Amalgamated East Anglian Brussels Sprout Company had overturned on its way to the market, and a heap of the little vegetables spread from one side of the road to the other.

And leaving the cabdriver thanking his lucky stars that they'd finished with his cab, they set off on foot, running as they'd never run before.

The ship's hooter sounded one long blast over the rooftops.

"Oh, no—" gasped Lily. "We'll never make it—"

"RUN!" said Spring-Heeled Jack.

On the ship, Mr. Summers had gotten dressed and come out on deck to watch as they left the shores of England behind.

The tug had brought the sharp end of the ship around to face the right way. The dock gates were open; the tide was at its height. Mr. Summers stood at the blunt end, leaning on the rail, looking back over the warehouses and the cranes and the rooftops as the ship moved slowly out of the dock.

Suddenly he stood up straight and rubbed his eyes. Leaping over the dock wall came a strange, devilish figure—and then, running in past the Customs shed, came a sailor with a suitcase, and one—two—three children . . .

The sailors on the tug avasted, and the tug stopped tugging.

And a minute or two later, the children were in the jolly boat, and so was Jim, and so was the suitcase.

And a minute or two after that . . .

But Spring-Heeled Jack had vanished.

The tide couldn't wait any longer. The sailors made fast
the capstans and broached the hawsers, and the ship
moved out into the busy river.

But we haven't quite finished with the streets yet.

Just at the very end of the night, a little wispy creature,
hardly visible, hardly there at all, could be seen (with a
little imagination) pulling at the sleeve of a certain weary
villain.

And around that corner—

Just then, who should come around the corner but the pieman.

And out on the ocean blue, the good ship *Indomitable* was steaming for the New World.